MY RIBBON SK

ISBN: 978-1719449496

Asini is my name.

My grandparents, my kokom and mossom, named me that. It means **Rock** in Cree. I am **Plains Cree**. My parents tease me and say I'm their rock, I think my name suits me. I am 10 years old. I have 2 big brothers and a little sister, I love them!

I love picking saskatoons with my mom. She always keeps me in her sight when we are out picking berries.

I THINK MY MOM IS **BEAUTIFUL!**

This is my room. I am taking my **ribbon skirts** out of my drawer.

My auntie made me two ribbon skirts
and my kokom made me one.

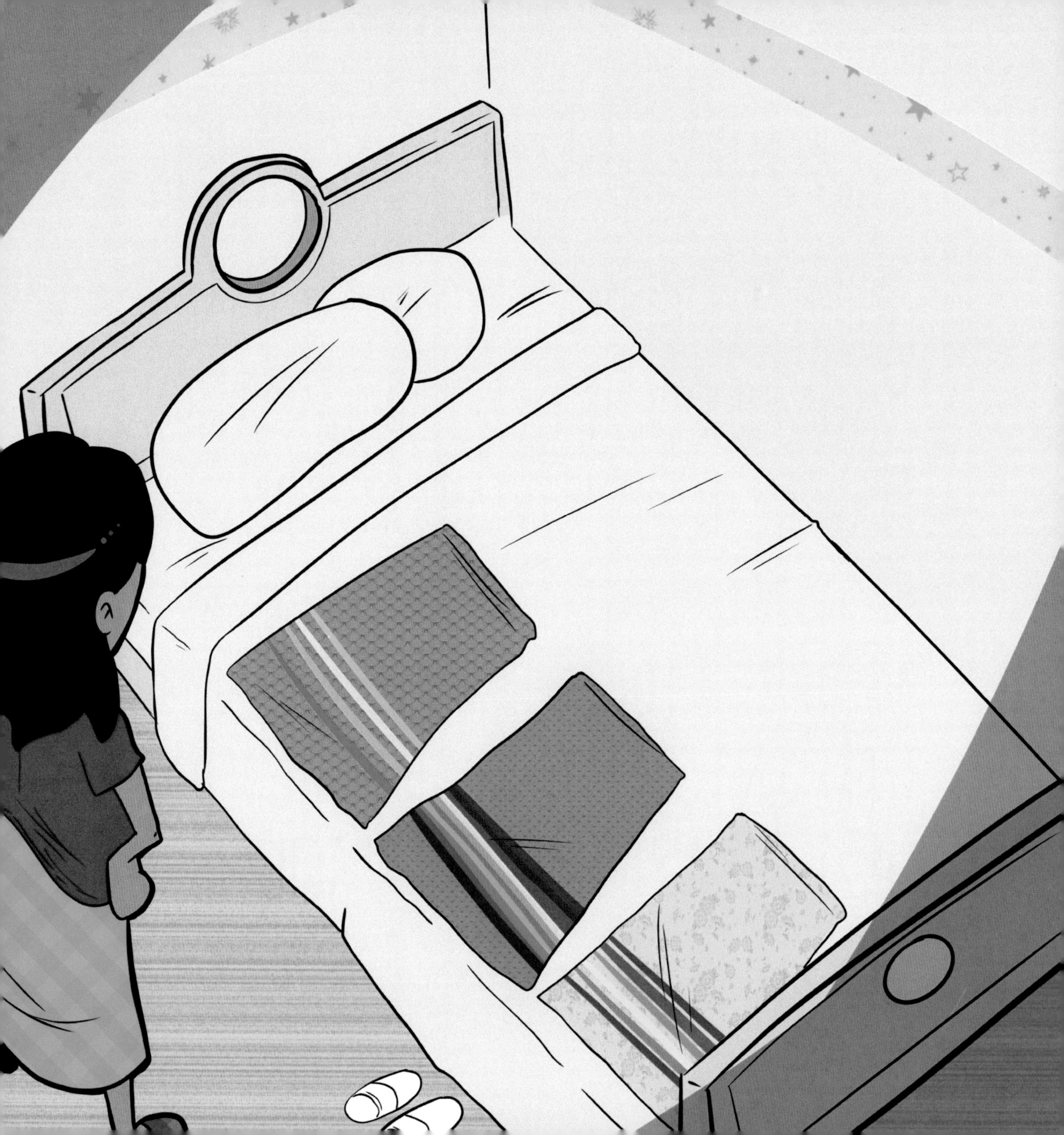

My auntie is my dad's sister.

We are going to a horse dance tomorrow! We picked Saskatoon berries to share with everyone there.

My auntie told me that ribbon skirts represent **strength** and **sacredness**. These are a part of our teachings. The pink skirt is my favorite.

My ribbon skirt also resembles a tipi.

My ancestors lived in tipis.
It was their home.

My auntie told me that there are fifteen teachings in a teepee.

Wearing my ribbon skirt reminds me of those teachings.

My ribbon skirt touches the ground when I walk. This is my connection to the earth. It reminds me that we must love the earth and I walk close to her.

I AM A LITTLE SISTER AND A BIG SISTER.
I KNOW MY FAMILY LOOKS UP TO ME AND
MY RIBBON SKIRT REMINDS ME OF THAT.
MY FAMILY IS IMPORTANT TO ME.

This is the ribbon skirt I chose.
My auntie made it for me.

The colors she used for the ribbons are my dad's favorite. My dad takes care of me. He is riding in the horse dance tomorrow.

See you again soon.
It's time for supper.

ABOUT THE AUTHOR

SHELLY NELSON

I WAS BORN IN PARADISE HILL, BUT, I CONSIDER EDMONTON, ALBERTA MY HOME. I WAS RAISED IN ONION LAKE, LOCATED IN CREE TERRITORY ON THE ALBERTA AND SASKATCHEWAN BORDER. I GREW UP LEARNING THE VALUES AND TRADITIONS IN MY COMMUNITY. I SPENT LOTS OF TIME OUTDOORS WITH MY FAMILY DOING NUMEROUS THINGS - LIKE BERRY PICKING, TAKING CARE OF HORSES AND LEARNING ABOUT RESPECTING THE LAND.

I'M THE MOTHER OF THREE BEAUTIFUL CHILDREN. LEARNING AND SHARING TRADITIONAL TEACHINGS IS A GUIDING PRINCIPLE I FAITHFULLY BELIEVE IN.

I'VE WORKED IN EDMONTON FOR YEARS, I ALSO SPEND MY TIME ATTENDING EVENTS SUPPORTING INDIGENOUS PEOPLES, CONCERTS, POW WOWS, EXERCISING IN THE RIVER VALLEY AND ALSO, ATTENDING MANY DIVERSE EVENTS IN THE CITY.

THANK YOU FOR READING MY BOOK.

MORE FROM EAGLESPEAKER PUBLISHING

AUTHENTICALLY INDIGENOUS NAPI STORIES:

Napi and the Rock
Napi and the Bullberries
Napi and the Wolves
Napi and the Buffalo
Napi and the Chickadees
Napi and the Coyote
Napi and the Elk
Napi and the Gophers
Napi and the Mice
Napi and the Prairie Chickens
Napi and the Bobcat
... and many more Napi tales to come

AUTHENTICALLY INDIGENOUS GRAPHIC NOVELS:

UNeducation: A Residential School Graphic Novel
Napi the Trixster: A Blackfoot Graphic Novel
UNeducation, Vol 2

AUTHENTICALLY INDIGENOUS COLORING BOOKS:

Napi: A Coloring Experience
UNeducation: A Coloring Experience
Completely Capricious Coloring Collection
A Day at the Powwow (grayscale coloring)

AUTHENTICALLY INDIGENOUS KIDS BOOKS:

Teeias Goes to a Powwow (a series)

WWW.EAGLESPEAKER.COM

**IF YOU ABSOLUTELY LOVED THIS BOOK (OR EVEN JUST KIND OF LIKED IT), PLEASE FIND IT ON AMAZON.COM AND LEAVE A QUICK REVIEW. YOUR WORDS HELP MORE THAN YOU MAY REALIZE.

Made in the USA
Coppell, TX
12 June 2021